This book of ABCs belongs to

_____

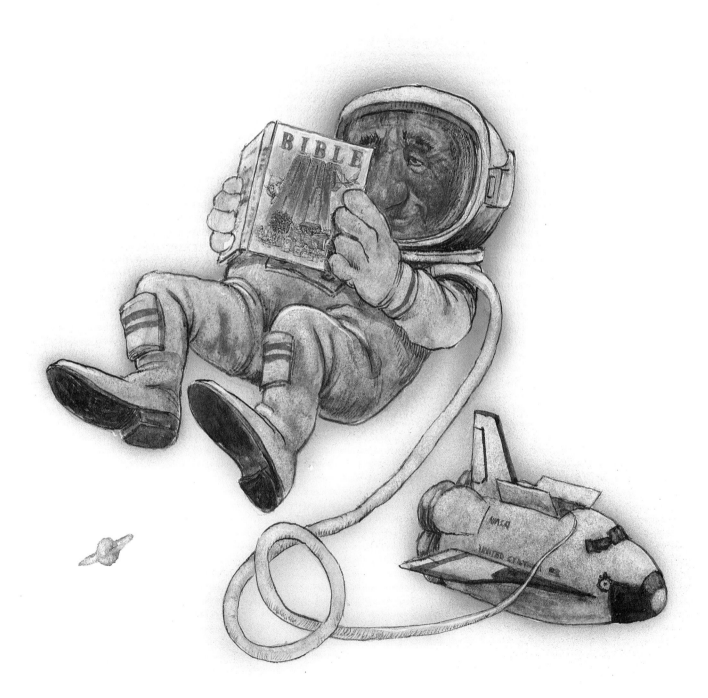

BIBLE ZOO

WRITTEN BY **Eric Metaxas**   ILLUSTRATED BY **Jim Harris**

Tommy NELSON

Thomas Nelson, Inc.

Nashville

Published in Nashville, Tennessee, by Tommy Nelson™, a division of Thomas Nelson, Inc.

Executive Editor: Laura Minchew
Managing Editor: Beverly Phillips
Project Editor: Lila Empson

Library of Congress Cataloging-in-Publication Data

Metaxas, Eric.
    Bible ABC / by Eric Metaxas ; illustrated by Jim Harris.
        p.   cm.
    Summary: Rhyming text and illustrations present a Biblical character for each letter of the alphabet.
    ISBN 0-8499-1524-4
    1. Bible—Juvenile literature. 2. English language—Alphabet—Juvenile literature. 3. Bible. [1. Alphabet.] I. Harris, Jim, 1955–   ill. II. Title.
BS539.M48   1998
220.3[E]—dc21

                                                                97-38515
                                                                CIP
                                                                AC

Printed in the United States of America

98 99 00 01 02 03 04 RRD 8 7 6 5 4 3 2 1

S is for Susanne, as is this book.

—E. M.

P is for parents—Mom, Dad, take a look!

—J. H.

${\large A}$ is for Adam, the first one of us,
Who ate a bad apple and caused quite a fuss.
So all of the errors you ever will make
Are the tragic results of poor Adam's mistake.

Based on Genesis 3

B is for Balaam, whose donkey spoke,
Which gave Balaam a shock, but was hardly a joke.
The creature had spared him from tasting God's wrath
From an angel of God who was blocking their path.

Based on Numbers 22

C is for Cain, Adam's first son,
Who angered the Lord with what he had done.
For killing his brother, he was banished by God
And lived, thenceforth, in the land of Nod.

Based on Genesis 4

D is for David, Israel's king,
Who slew Goliath with a shepherd's sling.
While playing the harp, he often found calm
By singing the words to a heavenly psalm.

Based on 1 Samuel 16, 17

E is for Esther, who lifted the gloom
Of her people, whom she saved from doom.
She pleaded with Xerxes, who heeded her cry,
And replaced Haman, the villain, with Mordecai.

Based on Esther 8

F is for the Foolish Virgins, five in all
Who forgot to bring the extra oil.
When the bridegroom shouted "Hark!"
The five of them stayed in the dark.

Based on Matthew 25

G is for Goliath, the giant from Gath,
Who challenged Israel and felt God's wrath.
He was arrogant and boastful, for his opponent was small,
But pride always goes before a fall.

Based on 1 Samuel 17

H is for Hagar, who bore Abraham's child,
A boy named Ishmael, rough and wild.
When Isaac was weaned, they were both sent away,
But the Lord watched over them every day.

Based on Genesis 16, 21

I is for Isaac, Abraham's son,
Whose birth made him marvel at what God had done.
It happened exactly as he had been told,
Though Abraham was a hundred years old.

Based on Genesis 18, 21

J is for Jesus, our Savior and Lord,
Our Joy and Messiah, the Incarnate Word.
He died to redeem us from Death and from Sin,
So when He comes knocking—*let Him in!*

Based on John 3

K is for Korah, who rebelled against God,
Causing the ground to open where he trod.
The Lord made a hole and Korah fell in,
And he wasn't heard from ever again.

Based on Numbers 16

L is for Luke, the Greek physician,
Who joined Paul the apostle on many a mission.
He wrote it all down (there are two books in all),
And that's how we know about Luke and Paul.

Based on Luke 1

M is for Moses, who at the Red Sea
Saw God lead His people to liberty.
They wandered for years in the hot desert sand
But arrived, in the end, at the Promised Land.

Based on Exodus 14

N is for Noah, who built a great boat
Before it had water in which to float.
The animals entered the ark in pairs
On a gopherwood plank for lack of stairs.

Based on Genesis 6

O is for Onesimus, a Colossian slave,
Whom Paul saw Jesus touch and save.
Thenceforth did Paul call him his son;
God frees His children, every one.

Based on Colossians 4

P is for Peter—his name means "rock"—
Who was given the care of his Master's flock.
He once was a fisher of fish, but then
Jesus made him a fisher of men.

Based on Matthew 4, 16

Q is for Sheba's noble Queen,
Who gave Solomon rubies and emeralds green.
She listened with care to his every word
And found heavenly wisdom in all that she heard.

Based on 1 Kings 10

R is for Ruth; though her husband died,
She vowed to stay by Naomi's side.
Boaz was moved by her great loyalty,
And they married and soon had a family.

Based on Ruth 1–4

S is for Samson, whose hair held his strength,
Provided it grew to a certain length.
It's good to be clean-cut and handsome,
But not to be clean-cut and Samson.

Based on Judges 13, 16

T is for Thomas, who doubted a lot
Until seeing he believed and doubted not.
Faith is not by sight, for eyes deceive;
Blessed are those who haven't seen, yet believe.

Based on John 20

U is for Uzziah, Judah's king,
Whose reign was blessed in everything.
But when this led to pride, you see,
Uzziah was struck with leprosy.

Based on 2 Chronicles 26

V is for Vashti, a prideful queen,
Whose stubbornness caused quite a scene.
When Xerxes called, she didn't budge
And found that he could bear a grudge.

Based on Esther 1

W is for the Wise Virgins, five in all.
They each brought jars of extra oil.
And so their lamps each had a flame
That burned until the bridegroom came!

Based on Matthew 25

X is for Xerxes, Persia's king,
Who sealed all proclamations with a signet ring.
Ahasuerus is his Hebrew name;
It's longer than Xerxes, but the height's the same.

Based on Esther 8

Y is for Yahweh, the King of Creation,
Whose love is cause for grand celebration.
He's heaven's sweet Monarch, both Lion and Lamb.
In Hebrew His name means "I AM THAT I AM."

Based on Genesis 1–2

Z is for Zacchaeus, who wasn't tall
And couldn't see in crowds at all.
But whenever he really wanted to see,
He'd climb atop a sycamore tree. *See?*

Based on Luke 19

Eric Metaxas grew up in Danbury, Connecticut, and attended Yale University, where he edited *The Yale Record,* the nation's oldest college humor magazine. He is former head writer for Rabbit Ears Productions, and his books have won numerous awards, including two Grammy nominations for Best Children's Recording.

His previous children's books include *The Birthday ABC* and *Uncle Mugsy and the Terrible Twins of Christmas.* Metaxas's humor pieces and book reviews have appeared in *The New York Times, The Washington Post,* and *Christianity Today.* He is currently an editor for *BreakPoint,* the radio ministry of Chuck Colson.

Jim Harris was born in Raleigh, North Carolina, and now lives and works in Mesa, Colorado, on the face of the world's largest flat-topped mountain. Harris's work has earned him the Communication Arts' Award of Excellence, four awards of merit, and a silver medal in the Society of Illustrators Annual Exhibition.

Harris has illustrated numerous books, including *The Three Little Javalinas,* which won the Arizona Young Readers Award and was a Reading Rainbow selection. His *Ten Little Dinosaurs* was featured on TV's *Good Morning, America* and appeared on *Publishers Weekly's* Top Ten Bestseller List for twelve weeks.

Where to find the original stories:

Adam—*Genesis 3*

Balaam—*Numbers 22*

Cain—*Genesis 4*

David—*1 Samuel 16, 17*

Esther—*Esther 8*

Foolish Virgins—*Matthew 25*

Goliath—*1 Samuel 17*

Hagar—*Genesis 16, 21*

Isaac—*Genesis 18, 21*

Jesus—*John 3*

Korah—*Numbers 16*

Luke—*Luke 1*

Moses—*Exodus 14*

Noah—*Genesis 6*

Onesimus—*Colossians 4*

Peter—*Matthew 4, 16*

Queen of Sheba—*1 Kings 10*

Ruth—*Ruth 1–4*

Samson—*Judges 13, 16*

Thomas—*John 20*

Uzziah—*2 Chronicles 26*

Vashti—*Esther 1*

Wise Virgins—*Matthew 25*

Xerxes—*Esther 8*

Yahweh—*Genesis 1–2*

Zacchaeus—*Luke 19*